D1220849

PROUD *as a* PEACOCK, BRAVE *as a* LION

JANE BARCLAY

Illustrated by RENNÉ BENOIT

TUNDRA BOOKS

Published in Canada by Tundra Books,
75 Sherbourne Street, Toronto, Ontario M5A 2P9

Published in the United States by Tundra Books of Northern New York,
P.O. Box 1030, Plattsburgh, New York 12901

Library of Congress Control Number: 2008909731

Library and Archives Canada Cataloguing in Publication

Barclay, Jane, 1957-
Proud as a peacock, brave as a lion / Jane Barclay ; Renné Benoit, illustrator.

ISBN 978-0-88776-951-1 (bound)

1. Remembrance Day (Canada)—Juvenile fiction.
I. Benoit, Renné II. Title.

PS8553.A74327P76 2009 jC813'.54 C2008-907098-4

We acknowledge the financial support of the Government of Canada through the Book Publishing Industry Development Program (BPIDP) and that of the Government of Ontario through the Ontario Media Development Corporation's Ontario Book Initiative. We further acknowledge the support of the Canada Council for the Arts and the Ontario Arts Council for our publishing program.

The illustrations for this book were rendered in watercolor and gouache

Printed and bound in Canada

1 2 3 4 5 6 14 13 12 11 10 09

To peace.
– J.B.

For Amelia and Emmett.
– R.B.

My poppa was a soldier.

When he was seventeen years old, he lied about his age so he could join the army and fight for our country in the war. I'm on his bed studying a picture of him in his uniform. His hair is too short and his pants are too long.

"Poppa," I ask him, "why did you lie about your age?"

"Well," he says, "so many other boys were joining, and I didn't want to be left behind. I couldn't wait to put on that uniform. As soon as I did, I felt as proud as a peacock!"

"Proud as a peacock?" I ask.

"Proud as that," he answers.

He struts across the floor with his chest puffed out and his belly pulled in. He stops in front of the mirror and combs his hair and pats some shaving lotion on his cheeks. He smiles at his reflection. But beneath my poppa's smile, I see the serious young man in the photograph.

My poppa crossed the ocean.

The war was far away, and he went on a long journey to get there. He said good-bye to his mom and dad and his sweetheart, Betty. He promised to write them letters every week.

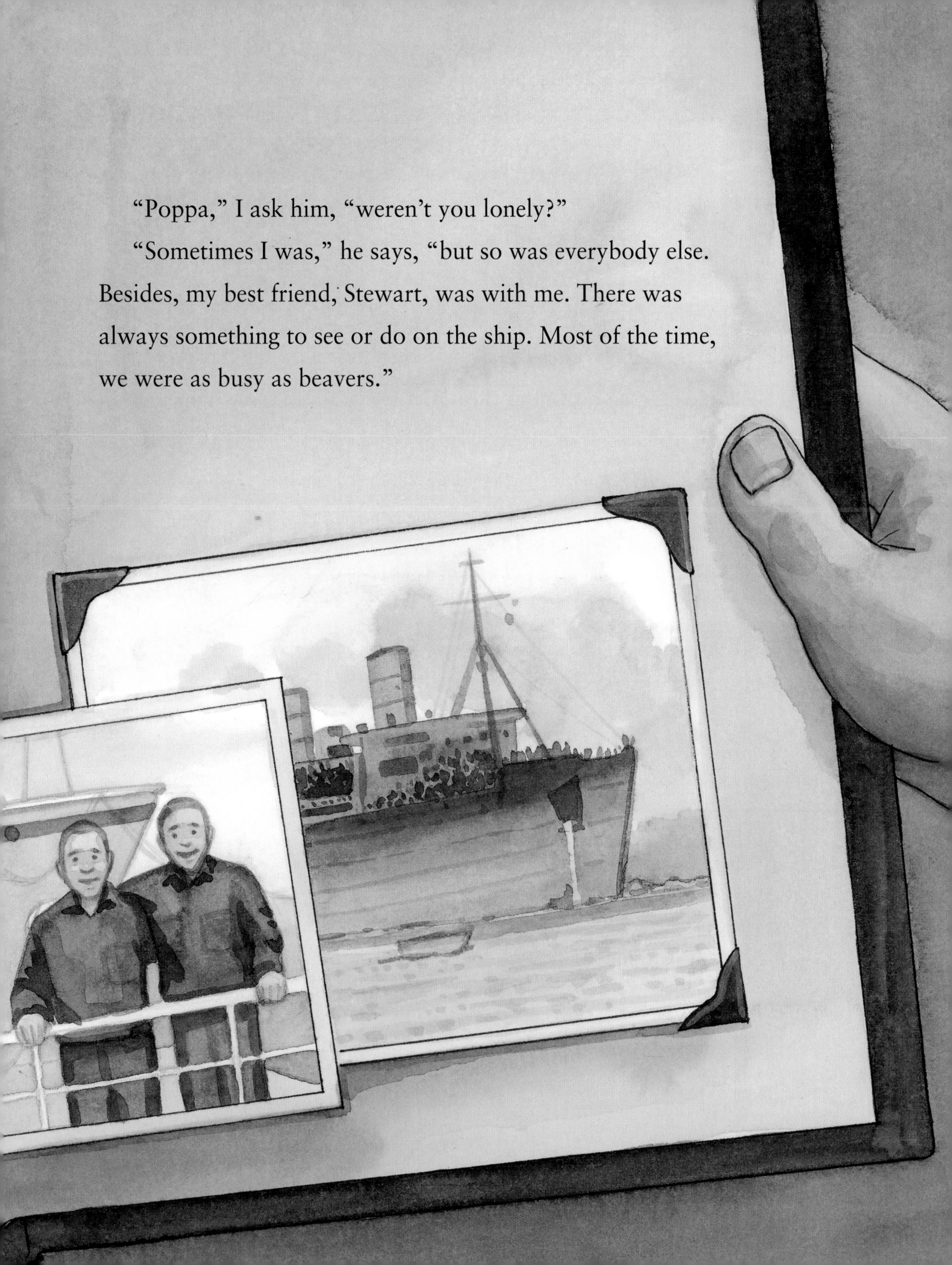

"Poppa," I ask him, "weren't you lonely?"

"Sometimes I was," he says, "but so was everybody else. Besides, my best friend, Stewart, was with me. There was always something to see or do on the ship. Most of the time, we were as busy as beavers."

"Busy as beavers?" I ask.

"Busy as that," he answers.

He whistles through his teeth as he irons his collar. He tucks in his shirttails and rubs the polishing cloth across his shoes until they shine like new. He reaches in the drawer for a pair of socks and I glimpse a bundle of letters tied with faded ribbon. He smiles as he touches it with his fingers. But beneath my poppa's smile, I know he's missing Grandma Betty.

My poppa was a hero.

There were guns and fire and smoke. He crawled on his belly through the noise and the mud and pulled three men to safety. The army gave him a special medal that he keeps in a leather case.

"Poppa," I ask him, "weren't you scared?"

"When I was a lad," he says, "I thought I wasn't afraid of anything. Then, when something frightening did happen, I pretended to be as brave as a lion."

"Brave as a lion?" I ask.

"Brave as that," he answers.

I help him fasten his medal above the pocket of his blazer. Sometimes my poppa's hands shake, so he needs to borrow mine. He smiles as he gives me a poppy to pin on my jacket. He looks very proud. But beneath my poppa's smile, I hear the bad dream that woke him in the night.

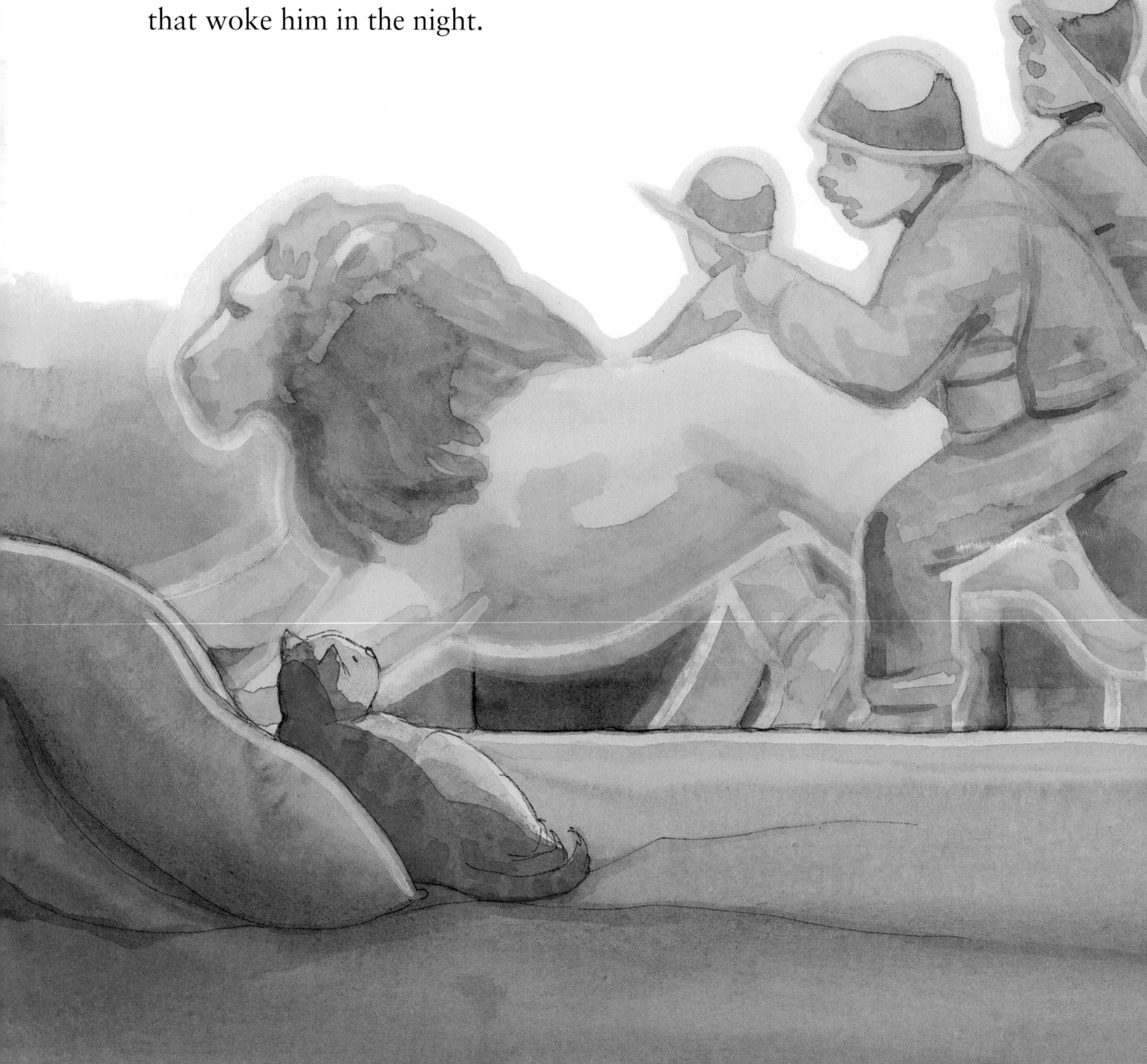

My poppa marches in the parade.

The crowd cheers and claps as the veterans go by. Some are young, some are old, some sit in wheelchairs, and some walk past, holding on to others. I stand at attention. The music stops, and there is a minute of silence. A cold wind sends dry leaves skittering past my feet.

I am as quiet as a mouse. As quiet as that.

My poppa lays a wreath.

He carefully places it at the base of the monument. Attached is a card that reads: "In loving memory of Stewart David Adams, 1923-1944." My poppa salutes, then he steps back and dabs his eyes with his handkerchief. He puts his hand over his heart. I do the same and I can almost touch the ache.

"Poppa," I whisper, "why are you crying?"

"I am remembering," he says. "A war is something you never forget."

“Elephants never forget,” I tell him.

“Then let’s be elephants,” he says.

A soft rain falls as a bugler trumpets his notes up into the cold, gray sky. We link our hands and bow our heads.